First published in the UK 2020 by Walker Books Ltd
87 Vauxhall Walk, London SE11 5HJ

Published by arrangement with Tundra Books, a division of Penguin Random House Canada Limited

2 4 6 8 10 9 7 5 3 1

© 2020 Anne Hunter

British Library Cataloguing in Publication Data:
a catalogue record for this book is available from the British Library

ISBN 978-1-4063-9378-1

www.walker.co.uk

Anne Hunter

Where's Baby?

WALKER BOOKS
AND SUBSIDIARIES
LONDON • BOSTON • SYDNEY • AUCKLAND

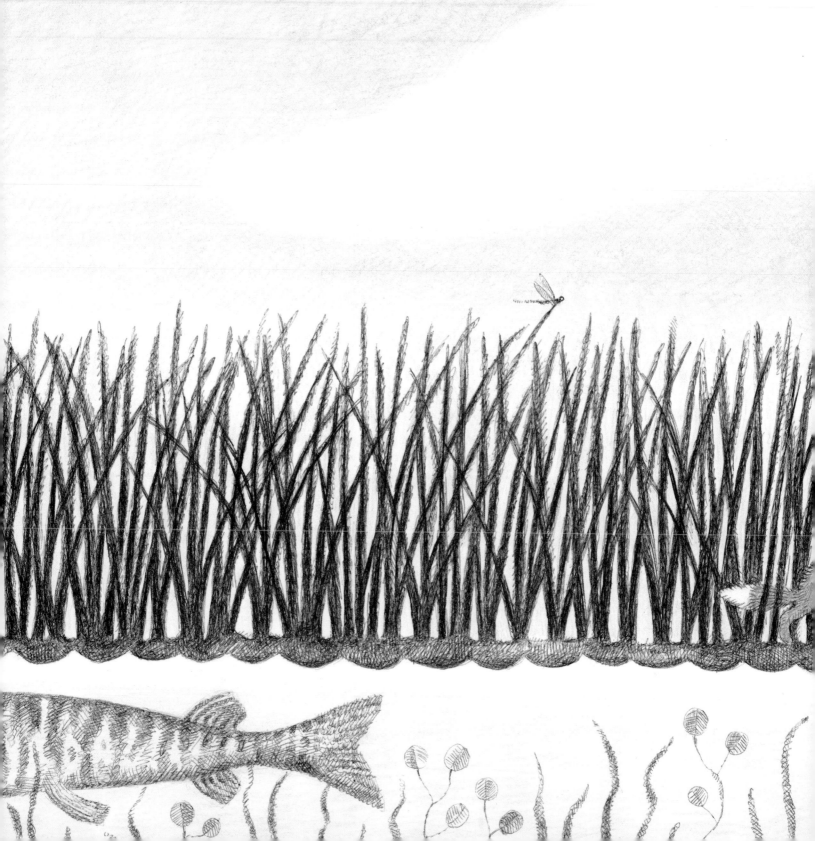

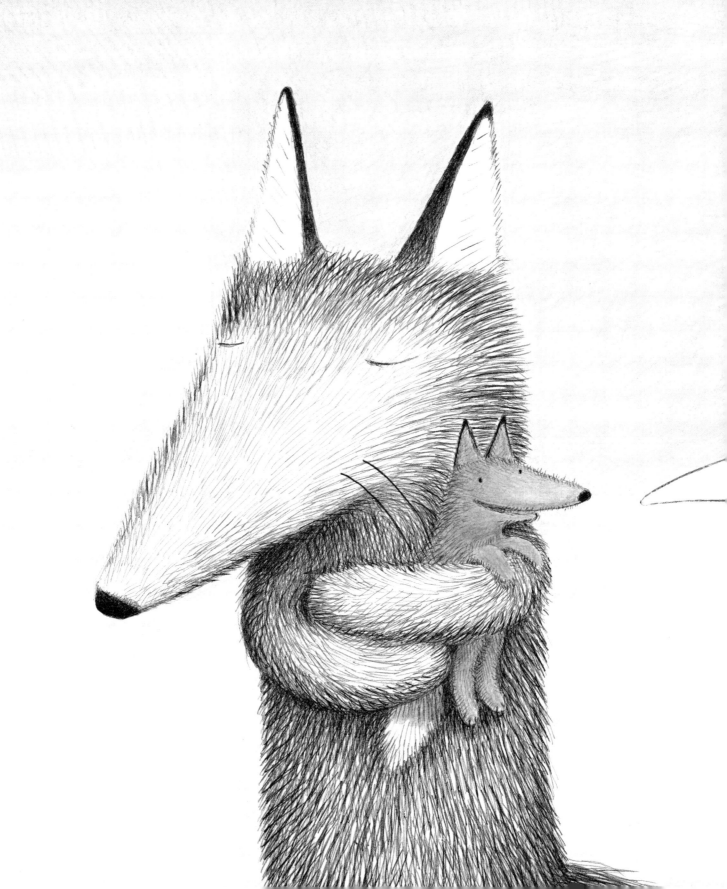

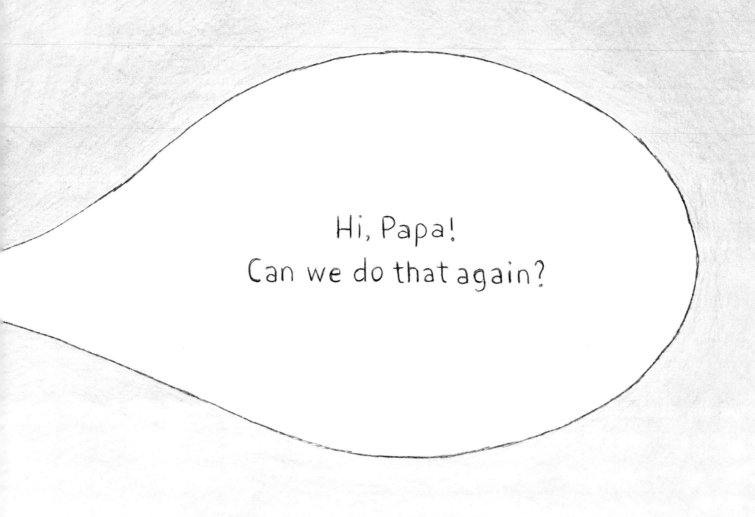